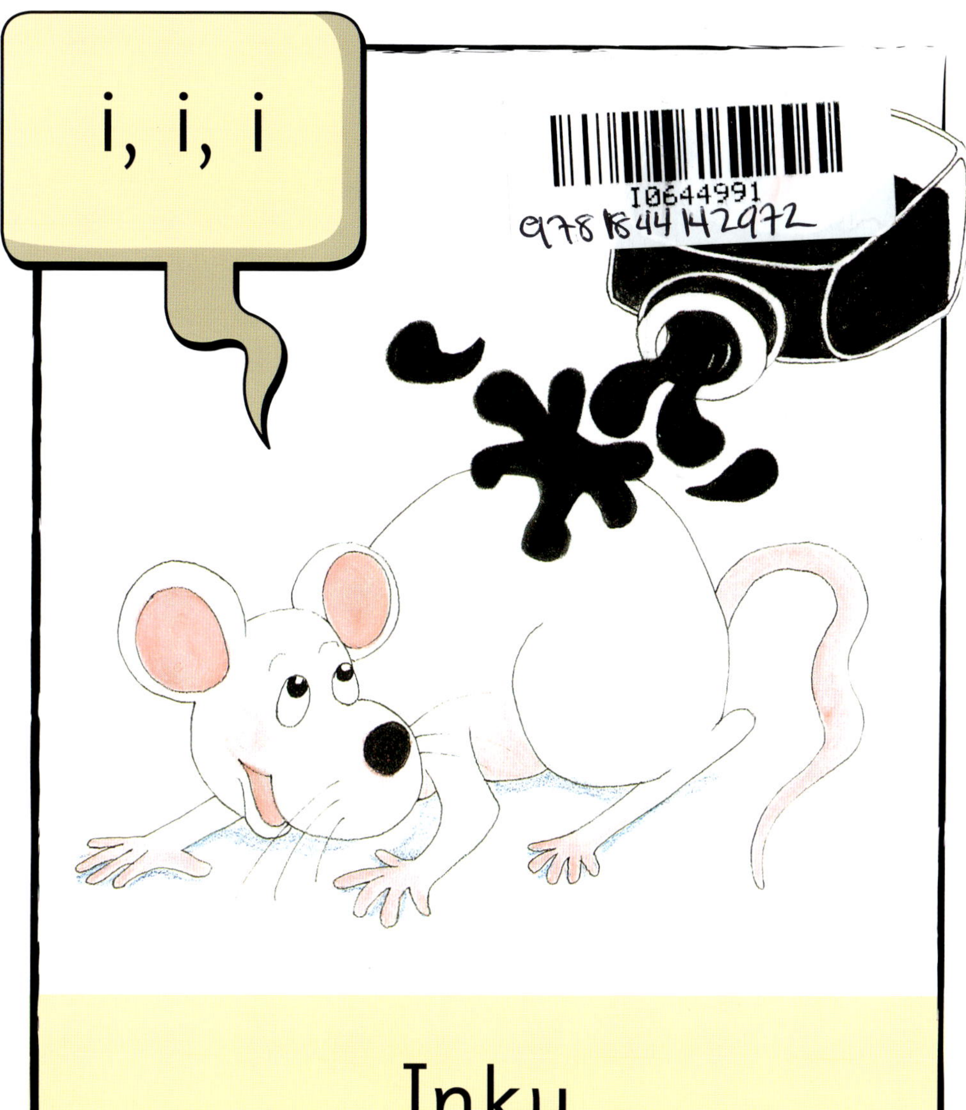

Inky

“i, i, i”

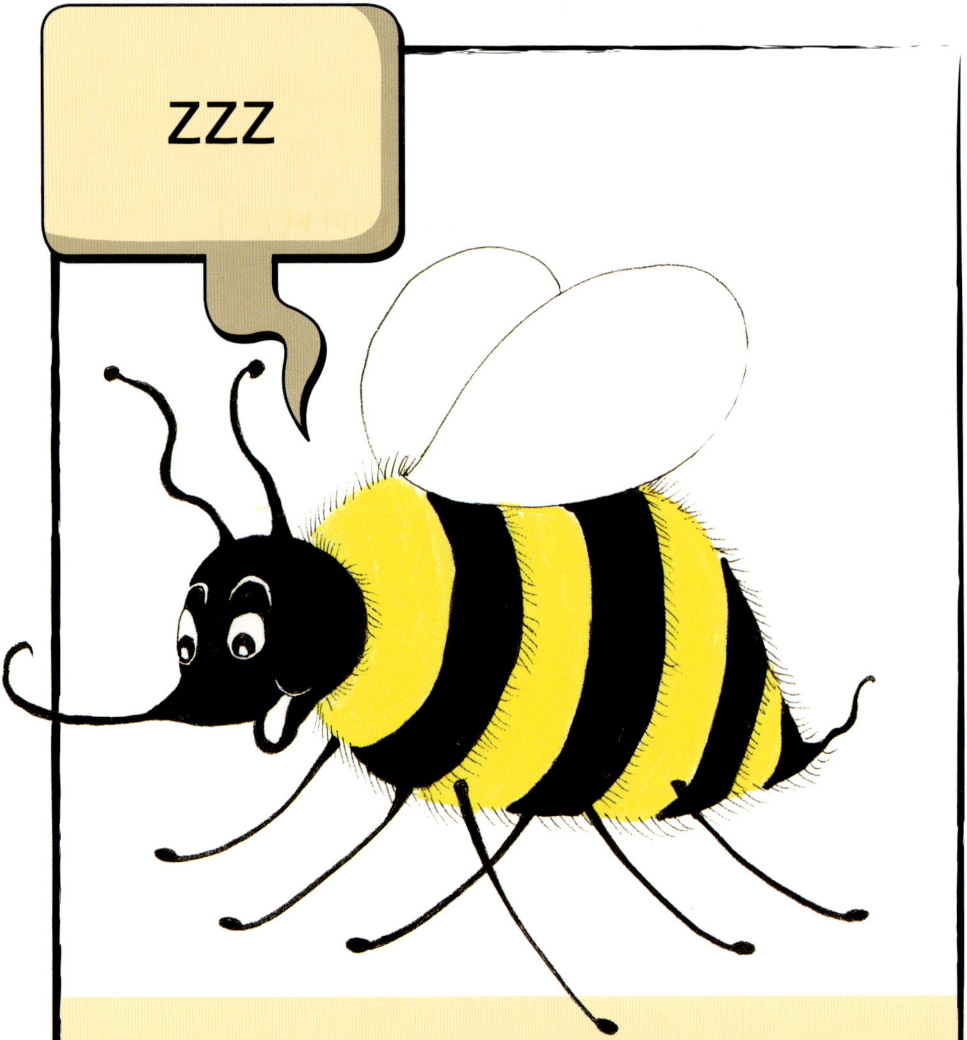

zzz

Bee

"zzz"

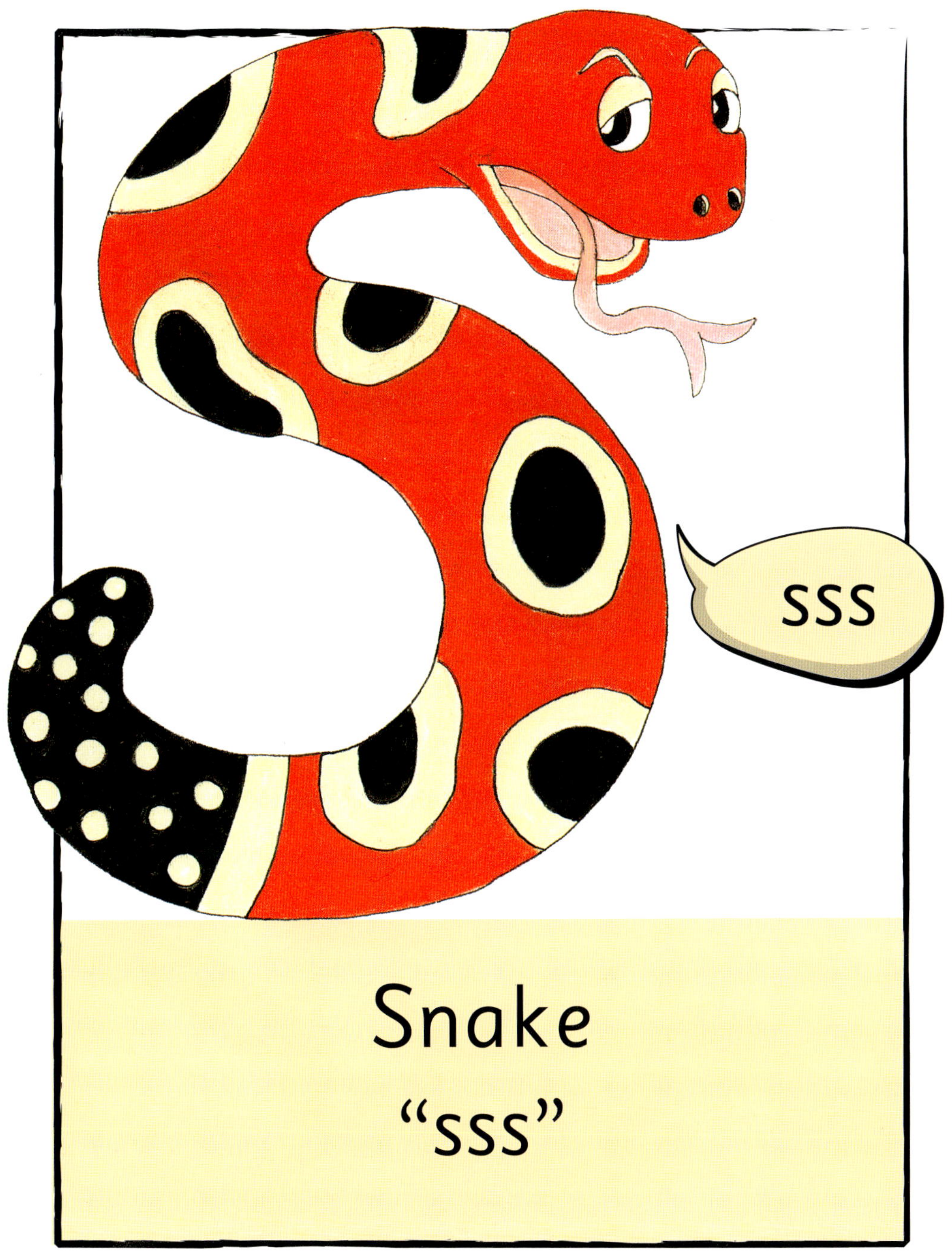

Snake

“sss”

Inky, Bee, and Snake run.

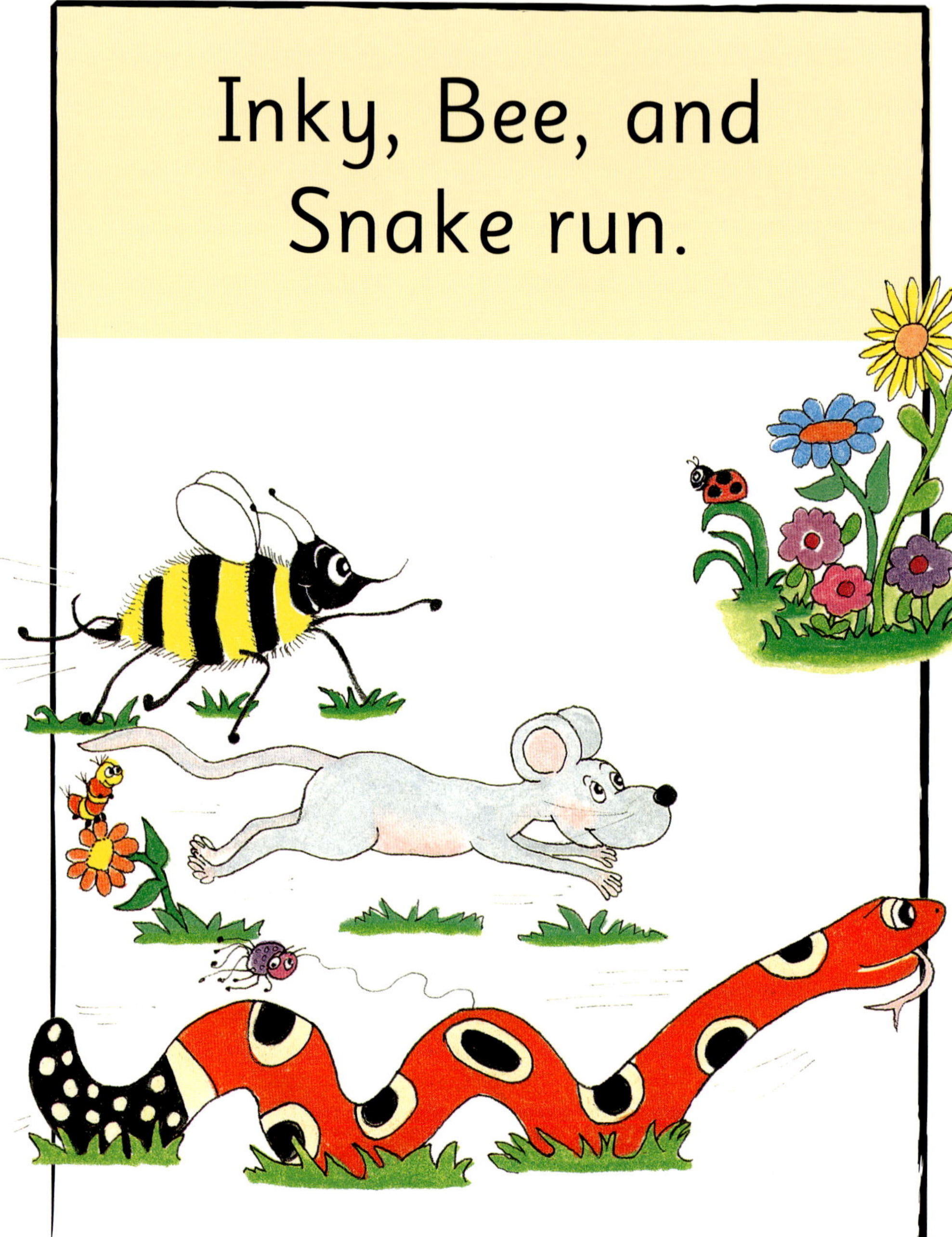

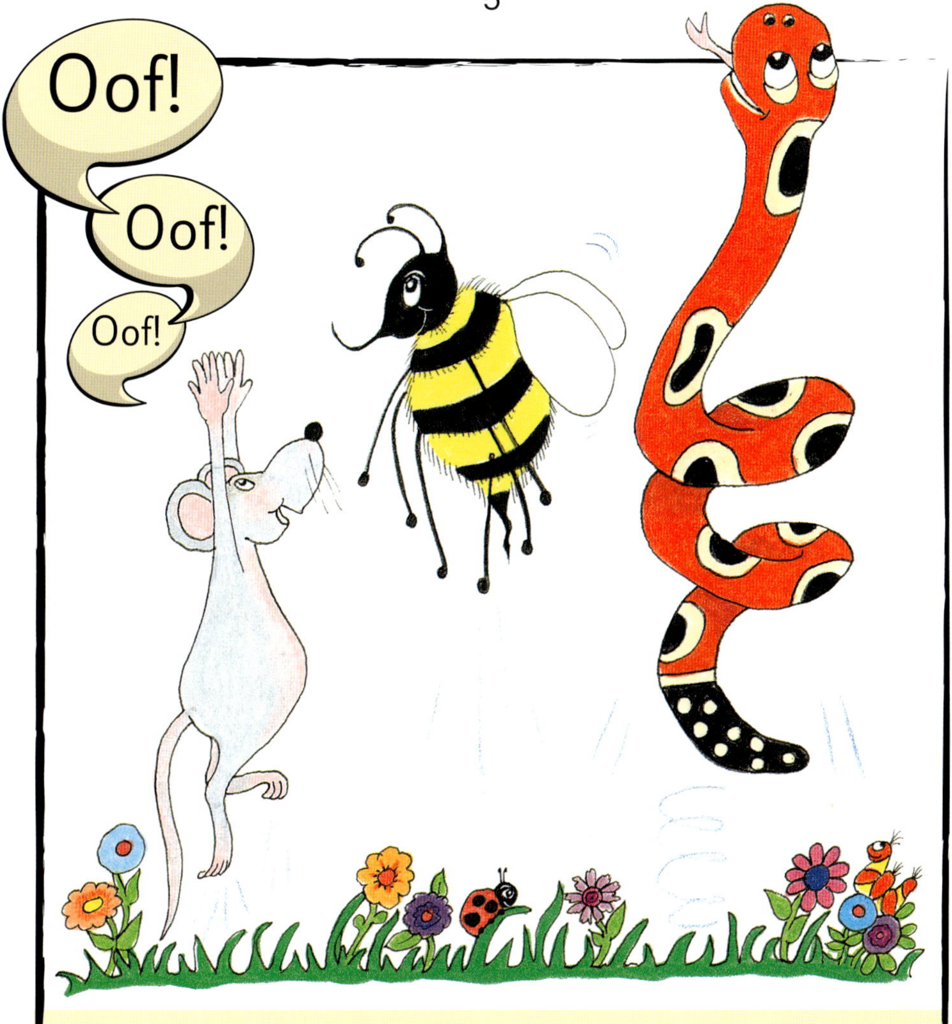

Oof!
Oof!
Oof!

Snake, Inky, and
Bee jump.

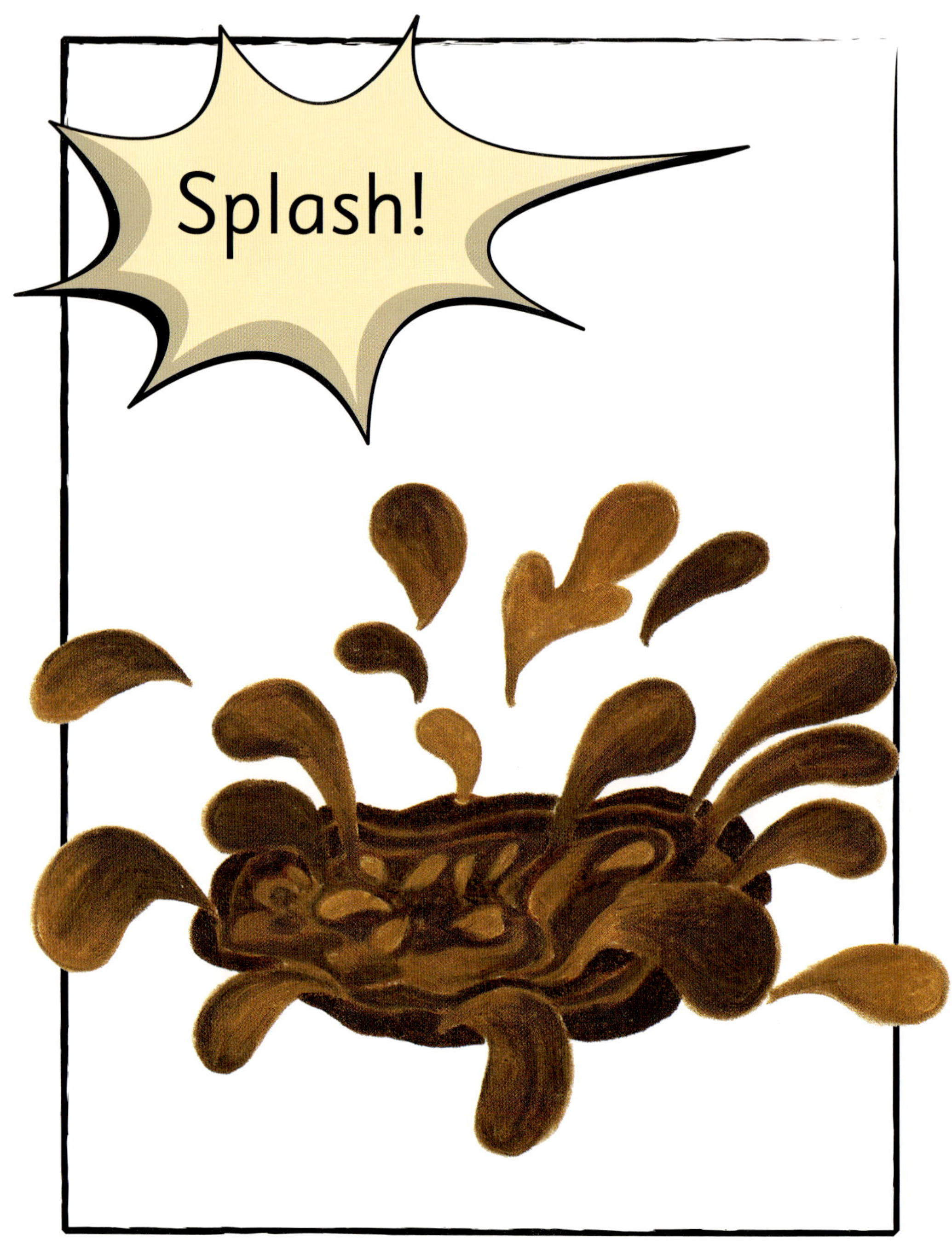
Splash!

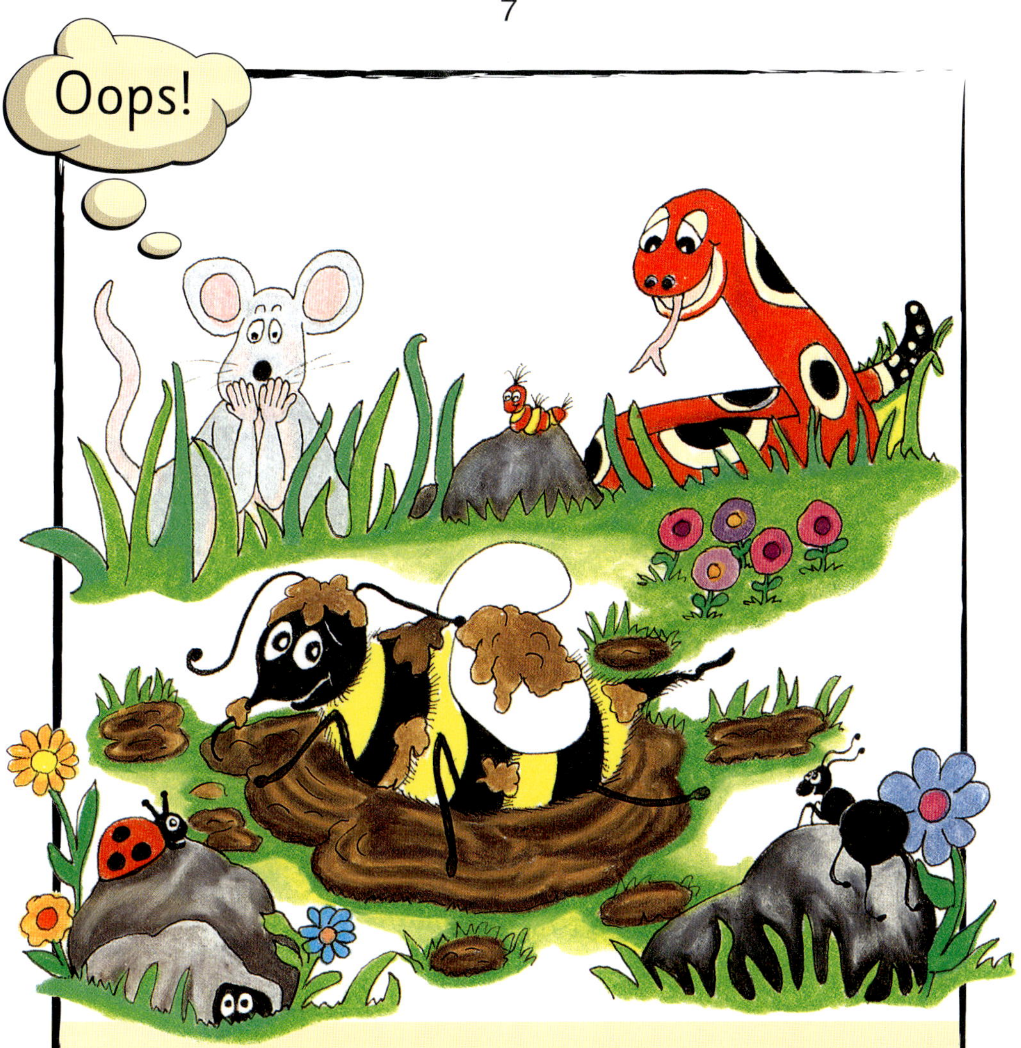

Bee lands in the mud.

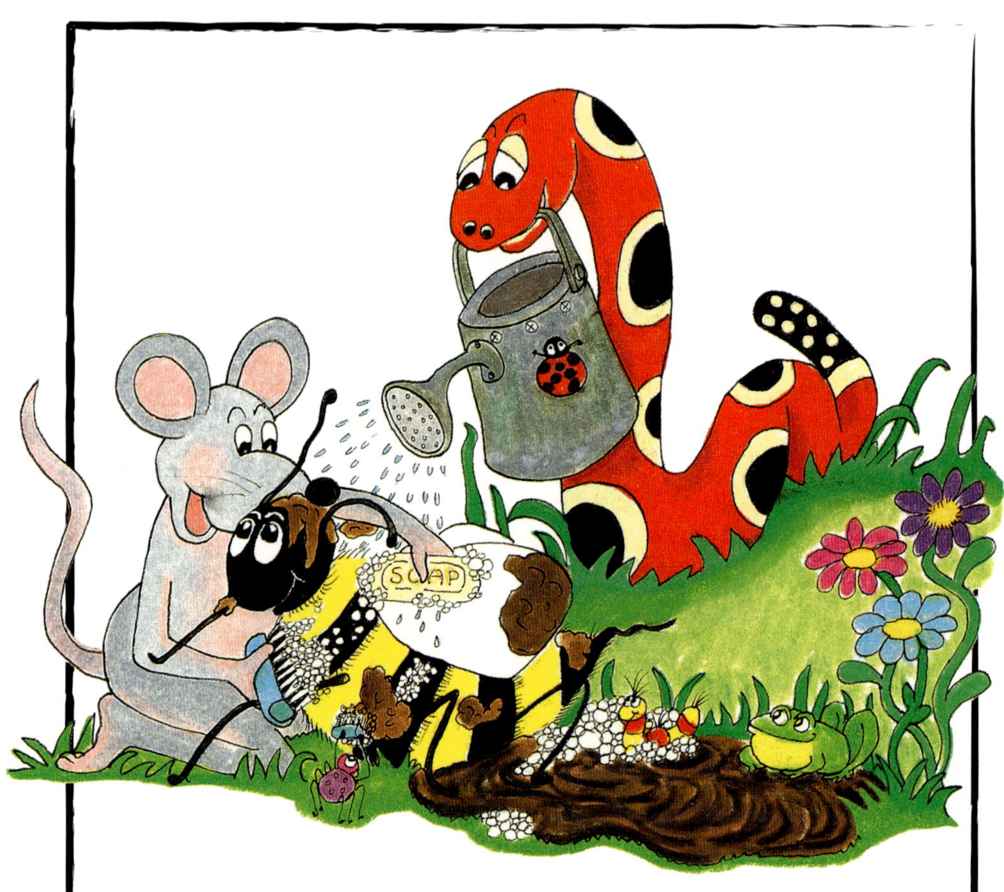

Inky and Snake help to scrub the mud off Bee.